BOUND BY FEATHERS, FREED BY LOVE

A ROMANTIC FANTASY OF CURSED LOVE AND DESTINY

SHIVANGI GOSWAMI

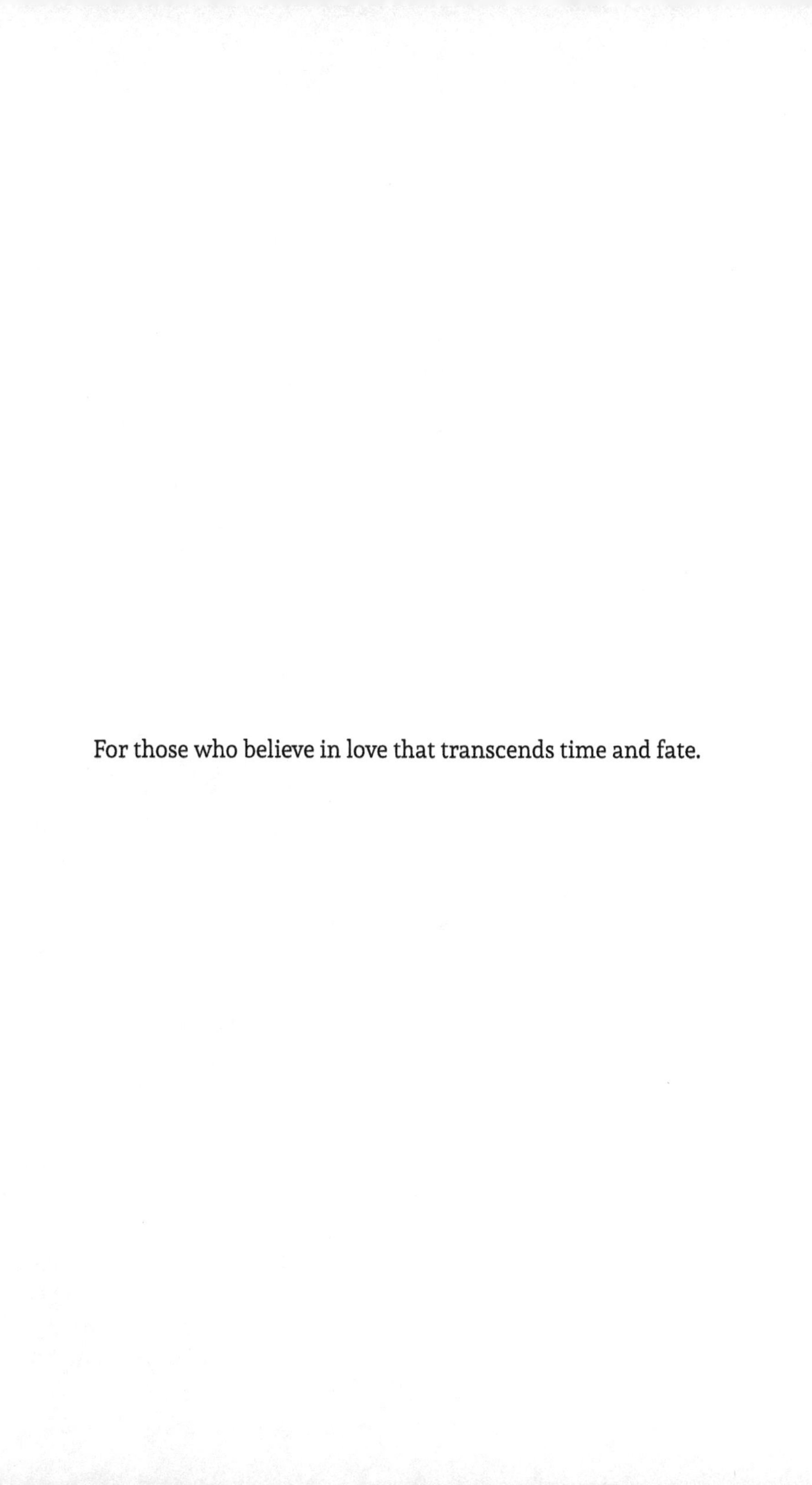

For those who believe in love that transcends time and fate.

Contents

Preface

Stories have always held a special kind of magic—the power to transport us to different worlds, to make us believe in the impossible, and to remind us that love transcends time and fate. Bound by Feathers, Freed by Love is one such story, born from my fascination with myths, destiny, and the deep connections that exist beyond words.

At its heart, this book is about love—the kind that withstands lifetimes, the kind that challenges fate itself. It is about longing, sacrifice, and the choices that define who we are. Amara and Syris' journey is one of discovery, pain, and, ultimately, hope.

This story started as a fleeting idea, a whisper of a tale that refused to leave my mind. As I wrote, it evolved into something much deeper than I had imagined—a story not just of romance, but of self-discovery and the strength that lies in trusting the unknown.

To every reader who picks up this book, thank you. Thank you for stepping into this world with me, for believing in stories that make hearts race and souls ache in the most beautiful ways. I hope this book brings you the same sense of wonder it brought me while writing it.

With love and magic,
Shivangi Goswami

Acknowledgements

Writing a book is never a solitary journey and I am immensely grateful to those who walked alongside me in this process. To my family and friends , your unwavering support and encouragement have been guiding light. To my readers, thankyou for your invaluable feedback and to every reader who picks up this book .

Thank you for stepping into this world with me.

ONE

THE QUILL OF SERENITY

The sky was filled with shades of gold and red, as if the sun had shown all its colour at once. Amara stood still, as she saw this mesmerizing view above her.

A soul of fire and light, wings through the sky, its wings spreading like molten lava against the fading sky. Feathers of gold and sun fire glowed , each one glowing that seemed almost alive. Its silver eyes met hers, sharp through the twilight, and in that moment, Amara felt something twitched within her, as if this being had been waiting for her since long.

Its voice, when it reached, was unlike anything she had ever heard. Not a voice, but a feeling—a melody murmured straight to her soul.

"You see me."

The world around amara faded. The air was spreading thick with warmness, yet she could not look away. For the first time, Amara wasn't scared of it.

And Syris... had finally found her.

But it wasn't just the view of him that held amara still, it was what she felt. A race of emotions flowed to her senses, raw and insecure, not her own but his.

Isolation, stretching across times. Yearning, so deep hurtled. With a weak hope, yet burning as boldly as the fire in his wings.

Amara's gift had always been loaded, forcing her to feel the emotions that were not hers, telling truths which no one else could hear.

She could feel the sorrow in dying leaves, the love in a mother bird's voice for her young ones. Every emotion in the world found a path into her heart.

But this...this one was something different. Syris was different. His soul didn't just speak to her; it had approached her, wrapping around her own as if it had been searching, waiting and longing for long.

At this time, Amara didn't try to let go of the emotions which she was feeling.

For the first time, she let herself feel them all.

"Who are you? Why do you want me to see you?" she asked, her voice barely carrying over the fading warmth in the air. She rubbed her eyes, heart pounding.

And when she looked again, the creature was gone.

"What was that? Why do I feel so drawn... as if I've known it forever?" Amara murmured, her feet moving before she could think.

She followed the faint, glowing path that ignited through the bushes, each step guided by an invisible force. And then, there it was.

A single golden feather, blooming brightly. It pounded with a soft, living glow, sparkling like a rare gemstone beneath the dusk.

Carefully, she picked it up. The moment her fingers wrapped around it, the feather shined brightly, its shine as if realising her touch.

Drawn by an unexplainable lust, she brought it close to her heart

And in that moment, the feather transformed. Light swirled around her like a whispered secret, shaping itself into a delicate pendant, warm against her skin, adorning her like it had always belonged there.

Amara kept searching around the jungle in the hopes of seeing that creature again. She began searching the area for signs that would help her find her way, but she was unsuccessful.

She inhaled deeply in frustration and peered down at the withered leaves underfoot. Normally, she would feel their quiet sorrow, the ache of life fading away. But now, at this time she felt nothing. No whisper of pain, no trace of emotion.

Her heart pounded. Her gift, her ability to feel the world's emotions, was gone.

Panic peaked through her mind. She rushed towards her home with a racing mind. Once reached, she pulled the pendant from around her neck and set it aside.

And just at that very moment, the flood of emotions returned to her. The emotions peaked back into her senses—the magic in the wind, the idleness of the night, the silent trees. The weight of it all pressed into her chest, suffocating.

Eager for relief, she took that pendant close to her heart. She felt the warmth and comfort instantly, soothing, silencing the flood of emotions.

A deep sigh escaped her lips as her body relaxed. For the first time, she felt peaceful from those emotions.

Before she could resist, sleep took —deep, uninterrupted, and more peaceful than anything she had ever experienced. Her eyelids become heavy.

TWO
WHISPERS OF UNKNOWN

Amara woke up to the warm glow of the lovely morning light passing in through her window. She blinked, her mind still heavy with sleep.

"Was it a dream?" Or am I simply overthinking things since I've always tried to avoid these emotions?"

Her empathy had been both a blessing and a curse since she was a child, a never-ending flood of feelings she couldn't turn off.

Perhaps, deep down, she had wished for silence. Maybe her mind had created the entire encounter with the fiery creature just to give her a reason to believe she could be free.

Shaking off the thoughts, she got out of bed, deciding to paint to clear her mind. The lake she had visited yesterday—before all the strange events—was the perfect subject. The still water, the golden sky at dusk... it was peaceful and familiar.

Lost in her thoughts, she took her things, completely forgetting about the pendant that is still resting against her skin.

Something didn't feel right as she was on her way towards the lake. Her surroundings around her were silent today but it wasn't the typical morning silence; rather, it was something else entirely.

Then, it hit her.

That strange, vacant emptiness.

She looked at the trees, the leaves, the earth beneath her feet—yet felt nothing. No gentle whisper of sorrow from fallen petals, no quiet joy from the rustling branches. The ever-present hum of emotions that had always been part of her existence was gone.

Her heart pounded as she knelt beside a wilting flower. Carefully, she reached out, forcing herself to connect, to feel.

Nothing.

It was just a flower, a mere object.

Cold realization crawled over her skin. Her gift, her curse, was gone. Or rather, something was suppressing it.

Her fingertips brushed against the pendant laying against her chest. A weird sensation pulsed under her hand.

" Was this... because of it?."

Amara ran toward the lake, annoyed by the nothingness that clung to her. Perhaps the wide sky, the calmness of the lake, and the soothing hum of the leaves would help her relax.

As she arrived, cool air touched through her skin, gently yet firmly, like a whisper she couldn't quite grasp. She closed her eyes for a time, allowing the emotion to wash over her.

It felt familiar, like a memory calling her back.

She set up her canvas and allowed her hands to move naturally. Colours merged smoothly with each stroke of her brush, creating unexpected shapes.

Time passed, and when she did take a step back, her breath stranded in her throat.

He was right there on the canvas. The creature of fire and light.

She had painted every feather in exquisite detail, with every glint of gold and amber intertwined into its form as if she had known it for years.

But how? She had only seen it for a second, yet the image on the canvas felt alive, as if she had captured something beyond sight.

Her hands trembled as she said, "How did I paint this?" "Where was I just now...?"

She leaned in and examined the painting closely. The creature's silver eyes contained something, a story, that she should remember.

And at that moment, the wind shifted again, this time stronger. As if the entire world was waiting for her to realize.

"Yes, I heard you."

Amara's words were barely a whisper, and her fingers trembled as they stroked the painted image. "Even if you didn't speak, I could hear you through this canvas. You've chosen me... as the companion of your love."

The wind swirled once more as the words left her lips, delivering a nice, musical song. The air around her was infused with unseen energy, wrapping around her like a loving hug.

"What a beautiful song, what a voice..." ."I have never heard anything like this before."

She got to her feet, her heart hammering with expectation, drawn in by the heavenly tune. She followed the music step by step, its haunting beauty taking her deeper into the woods.

And suddenly she noticed something. Something that would change everything.

THREE

THE UNSPOKEN BOND

Amara's heart raced as she held the creature's gaze, searching for answers in those silver eyes. But she felt something as if they were hiding a reality that they weren't ready to share.

"Why am I so connected to you?" she asked, her voice filled with fear.

The creature didn't answer. Rather, it stretched its golden wings, illuminating the cave like a rising sun. It moved closer, its presence both calming and overwhelming, as if it carried the weight of an unspoken truth.

Then it gently swiped one of its shining feathers across her hand. A soft but powerful warmth rushed through her, gushing into her skin like a quiet promise.

She gasped.

The small cut on her palm vanished. And then, as the feather traced over her wrist, she felt a magical sensation. Her birthmark also disappeared as if it had never existed.

Her fingers trembled over the now unblemished skin.
" What... but how? "

She looked up at the creature, her lips parted in astonishment. It had healed her, not just her wound, but a part of her she had carried all her life.

A silent understanding passed between them. It was growing attached to her. She could feel it, just as deeply as she felt its hesitation, its conflict.

Something was holding it back.

There was something, keeping it from completely sticking with her.

And before she could say another word, the creature turned away, its brilliant form disappearing into the cave's depths.

Leaving Amara alone with more questions than ever.

"No, not again!" Amara's voice echoed across the cave, with dissatisfaction in her words. She grasped her hands and glanced around for the bright thing. But it had vanished, just like before.

The emptiness of the cave rushed across her chest, as if the very air carried some sorrow. She took a deep breath, trying to steady herself.

Her eyes settled on the rough walls that surrounded her, with faint paintings carved on walls of the cave.

Symbols, patterns and drawing that faded with time, others still bright. " Are they some messages or clues that are left behind ? "

She moved closer, touching over the paintings. They pulsed faintly beneath her touch, creating an odd shiver in her body.

"What are they implying?"

A thought struck her.

She removed the pendant from her neck and as it left her skin, a familiar surge of emotions returned to her.

Kneeling on the chilly ground, she ran her fingertips over the soft moss that grew at the cave's entrance.

"Tell me," she said, her voice barely audible.

"What is going on? What's the truth ? What has been hidden?"

The wind outside shifted, rustling the leaves beyond the cave. The trees swayed, their silent voices brushing against her thoughts. The flowers at her feet trembled, and for a brief moment, she could feel their sadness.

A single message weaved itself into her senses.

"He is trapped... Between what he was and what he must become."

Amara's breath hiked.

"Trapped?" she whispered, holding a nearby vine for support.

The plants around her didn't say anything further, only humming with an energy she couldn't yet decipher.

She looked down at the pendant resting in her palm. It still glowed faintly, warm with the lingering touch of the creature's magic. " Was this the key? Was she meant to free him?"

A new determination filled her chest.

No matter what it took, she would find out the truth.

"Wait, what are you thinking, Amara?" she murmured to herself, holding the edges of her chair.

"It's just a beautiful bird."

She shook her head, trying to silence the peak of emotions dwelling inside her. " How can you fall for such a creature, whom you don't even know well"

She looked back at the painting, at the way her own hands had unknowingly captured every detail of the creature.

"No, this isn't normal. It's absurd."

A bitter chuckle escaped her lips. " The town already thinks I'm mad because of my empathetic nature. If they find out I've fallen for a bird, they'll drag me straight to a mental hospital."

She buried her face in her hands, in disappointment

But no matter how much she tried to deny it, she couldn't ignore what she felt deep within.

Not fear. Not confusion.

But trust.

She trusted him—this strange, ethereal being more than she had ever trusted another soul.

And no matter how impossible it seemed, she trusted her love for him more than anything else.

FOUR

SHADOWS OF HIDDEN PAIN

She went back to the cave after leaving her home, hoping to catch a glimpse of the bird once more. She stood patiently, her eyes scanning every movement and shadow in the area. But however long she waited, the creature never showed up.

She looked aside, when she could no longer find any trace of it. As she was dying out of thirst, she walked towards a river. As she arrived at the bank of the river, her disappointment was converted into wonder.

"What a heavenly spot this is," she uttered. The chattering of leaves and the distant chirping of birds made music in the air. Even the deer that fed near her seemed to delight in her presence.

"I might stay here forever," she whispered softly, content with herself.

There was a lovely musical trill at the moment. Her heart ceased in her realization.

"It's him !"

It was mesmerizing, it drew her along. Unconsciously, she moved following the voice.

"Is that the way you show me the path?" she thought, and a soft smile spread upon her lips.

"Well, no matter what it is, I shall seek you, again."

Finally, she saw him.

The bird sat upon a flowering rose, his feathers glinting in the sunlight, so brilliant that it robbed her of her breath.

She crept cautiously, not wanting to risk making even the quietest step for fear that it would make him disappear again.

"You're back," she whispered, barely making a sound louder than the creaking leaves.

The bird's sweet singing song died as it glanced back at her, its silver eyes filled with a feeling which she could not fathom

There was a soft wind that touched her, carrying the warmth in it. The pendant at her chest throbbed gently, as though answering his presence.

"Why do you always vanish?" she asked, cradling the pendant as though it held secrets she was trying to discover. "Every time I think I'm understanding you, you vanish like a dream."

The world around her distorted and glowed.

And before, she could take a second breath, the entire scene shifted.

"Stop playing with my feelings! I see this is merely an illusion you weave to raise the burden of my pity," Amara exploded, her voice shaking with emotion.

Her fists were balled as she advanced. "You are no common bird, are you? I can tell you are keeping something from me."

Silence descended upon them. The bird's once bright silver eyes turned sorrowful.

Amara's tone turned to worry as she noticed the change in his expression. She spoke softly, "I didn't mean to hurt you," taking a deep breath.

"I'm just worried about you. What kind of pain you're experiencing and Why do you keep it inside?"

The bird said nothing, but she could feel his sorrowfulness and hesitation.

She continued, "Mostly, people say that God has created someone for everyone in this world. I believe it was not a coincidence when we met, but fate. I think we were meant to be together."

She went on, "I know there is something between us that I just cannot say and I do not know how to determine what the honest truth is, but I do feel my instincts."

The bird's silver eyes flashed with an instant, unspoken emotion at her words that vanished immediately. He let out a soft breath, hiding the turmoil in his emotions.

"It's just that you sense the feelings of all living creatures on this earth," he said, his voice judicious. "So tell me, Amara. Do you feel my feelings?"

She locked eyes with him, seeking the truth he was unwilling to say.

"There is nothing unique about me or us," he went on, trying to sound hollow with laughter. "Perhaps it's simply my radiant feathers that drew your attention. Maybe you're only drawn to how I look."

His laugh was faint, yet she could feel the pain which he attempted to conceal.

"Oh, that's what you truly think?" Amara said in an offending tone "Do you believe I am a fool? I hear and feel the feelings of all living things since childhood like the pain of dead leaves, the joy of a sprouting flower. I do not see them, I feel them."

She came in closer and told him "This is not just attraction. If it were, then tell me, how am I supposed to hear your chirping when, to everyone else, it is only a melody? I hear all the words that you speak, I feel the pain you so desperately hide."

Syris puffed out his gleaming feathers, his silver eyes veiling. "You're thinking too much," he snapped. "Don't get caught up in this fantasy, Amara. Stop looking for me, I can't be everywhere at once."

He didn't let her reply, unfurling his wings and lifting into the air, leaving her to stand alone with words unspoken.

She gripped her fist so hard and said "You may fly wherever you please," she screamed out in anger, "but I will catch you again."

Amara stood up on her feet, her eyes burning with anger. If he won't admit the truth to me, I'll find it out myself.

And thus, with moonlight ascending above her, she set out to heed the summons of destiny, wherever it may lead. With the pendant clutched against her neck, she breathed in deeply, her resolve firming.

"No distance can keep us apart, Syris. I will come for you."

Embracing that promise in her heart, Amara braved the unknown, ready to follow the truth hidden in the whispers of the wind.

FIVE

THE SECRET BURIED IN TIME

Since, then amara follows every sign, to find the truth about syris, hoping to find something, that will lead her closer to him.

It was on a fine evening, when the sky was coloured in shades of violet and gold, she went to an old lake nestled deep in the woods where the water sparkled, reflecting the stars even before they could be seen in the sky. Attracted to its beauty, Amara kneels by it, dipping her fingers into the icy water.

A soothing ruffle is created, but before she can act, a moon-white swan moves gently towards her, its eyes filled with an indescribable sorrow.

"You carry questions in your heart," the swan speaks, its voice echoing like a forgotten melody.

Amara gasps. "You can speak?"

The swan nods and says "And I have a truth to share, one that has been buried in time."

Hearing those words, Amara's heart pounds. Could this creature know about Syris?

The swan looks toward the horizon as if lost in memories. "The bird you seek... he is not just a bird. He is a lost soul, bound by a curse. I once cast a moment of blind rage."

"A long time ago, in a time that is lost to history, I was not simply a swan, I was a guardian of the waters, and he was not always a bird.".

" He was young, sweet, and life-filled. He wandered about freely in the forest, like you do currently, his heart having never seen misery. But one fateful day, everything changed.

I had a mate, my beloved, who was my soul, my other half. We swans love only once in our lifetime, and when we do, it is eternal.

But one cruel evening, hunters entered these sacred woods. Their arrows tore through the air, piercing the silence—piercing lives.

When I arrived, my mate lay still, his wings spread across the ground, his lifeblood staining the earth. And standing near him, a figure—bow in hand, eyes wide with shock.

I was blinded by grief and by rage. I did not stop to see the truth.

I spoke the curse before he could utter a word."

'If you have stolen my love, then so shall yours be taken from you. You shall live, not as a man, but as a creature of the skies, bound to endless rebirths until the day love truly sets you free. Until then, you will suffer, knowing neither peace nor rest.'

" I watched as his body twisted, his cries turning into the cries of a bird. Feathers bloomed where flesh once was, and his silver eyes—once filled with warmth—dimmed with sorrow. He flapped his wings for the first time, not in freedom, but in agony.

I thought I had avenged my mate.

But I was wrong.

Days went by, then years, and the truth crept up on me like a wicked whisper. The hunter who killed my beloved was another—a shadowy figure invisible among the trees. The lad I cursed had been innocent.

But curses, once uttered, cannot be withdrawn."

The voice of the swan trembled as she went on, "My remorse became my weight, yet I could not leave him to suffer utterly. If I could not reverse my words, then I could alter his destiny at least.

And so I bestowed upon him something no ordinary bird could have—supernatural abilities, powers beyond those of any beast hitherto. He would not be locked in one form, nor would time age him like it would for other birds".

" But the suffering... the suffering of being caught in a cycle of life and death, with no peace to be found—that I could never remove. That, only love could shatter."

The swan stood before Amara, her very old eyes sorrowful. "And so, he wanders, lifetime upon lifetime, between hope and despair, awaiting the one who will release him."

Amara's breath suspended. "And what if he never does?" she whispered.

The swan lowered her head. "Then he will continue being born, again and again, to the end of time."

Silence lay between them, heavy with the weight of the past. Amara's fists were balled.

No. She never accepted that fate.

Syris would not last forever. She would find a way of breaking the curse.

No matter what it took.

SIX

UNDER THE STARLIT SKY

Amara sat by the riverbank, observing the water dance under the pale moon. The stars above sparkled like small secrets scattered in the darkness, and each one of them whispered tales of destiny and yearning.

"If Syris knew everything, then why did he not tell me?" she whispered, her voice barely more than the leaves.

He had known that she might help him. He had known that she was the one he waited for across lifetimes, across uncountable rebirths. And still he had not told her.

Her fingers made patterns on the mud at her feet. Why had he been so obscure for so long? A spirit with sadness and with resilience, tied up in a history he would not share.

"You don't deserve to love me, Amara."

She could already hear them from his lips, far and distinct, as if they had always been for her.

But Syris did not deserve this destiny. He did not deserve this agony he'd had to suffer.

And if he would not surrender, she would go to shatter the walls he had erected.

Amara approached the cave, her steps light but hesitant. She stopped beside the tree that stood just beyond it, its trunk smoothed to a sheen where Syris used to sit.

Closing her eyes, she whistled his song always—the melody that contained sorrow and longing.

There was a soft chirp broken.

"You're off by a note," Syris corrected, his voice weaving into the night like a whisper of wind.

He perched on a low branch, tilting his head as he continued the song, filling the air with its haunting beauty.

Amara smiled. "Such a lovely voice you have," she whispered, "and yet you still refuse to speak from your heart."

Syris fluffed his feathers, his eyes flying up to the heavens. "You're overthinking this, Amara. There is nothing to say."

"If that's the case, then why is it that I heard you've constructed walls around your heart? You keep it locked up and don't let anyone in?"

"You think too much." There was a tease to his voice, and something else beneath it—a sharpening warning.

"I am just a bird who sings of the sky and the stars. I wander, I trill. I do not search for anything. least of all love. "

"I am not a person, Amara."

She took a step closer, her gaze unwavering. "And yet, I've also heard that your heart was once broken. That's why you've locked it away, leaving no window open for love to slip through."

Syris fell silent.

For a fleeting moment, his wings trembled, as if carrying a weight far heavier than the night breeze.

Syris stood stock still, his eyes empty space. The stars shone in his golden eyes, but there was something that softened their glint.

Amara waited, she could feel the struggle inside him—the ruffling of his feathers, the tight clutch of his talons on the bark.

Finally, he spoke. His voice was little more than a whisper.

"You're right, Amara," he admitted, his voice heavy with a pain she had yet to hear. "I've constructed walls across my heart, not because I want to, but because I have to."

She drew in a breath, calming herself. "Why?"

Syris rotated his head to her, his eyes burning with something raw, something fragile. "Because I'm not supposed to love you, Amara."

A blinding pang hit her chest. "But you do."

Syris gave a cynical laugh. "Aye," he admitted, his voice laced with the weight of centuries.

"I love you. I have for longer than I should have let myself. But what sort of love is this? I am tied to the winds, a terror forced to inhabit a body which never was mine to start. And you—" He coughed on his own attempts at speech.

"You're human. You're of the world of heat and life, of hands to hold and lips to whisper promises. I can't give you that, Amara."

She tilted her head, her body from side to side. "Love isn't what body we're in, Syris. It's how we feel. How we give."

"But you can't love me," he said

"How do I go out and find a human to be my friend? How do I give you a life when I am not even of this world as you are?" questioned syris.

Amara's heart hurt, as she said "Then why do you stay?"

Syris painted. "Because no matter how much I struggle against it, no matter how much I struggle to convince myself that I shouldn't... I can't leave you behind."

They stood there in a silence heavy with unsaid words and the hushed rumble of night.

Amara's fingers touched him, stroked him, and traced the lines of his feathers.

"Then don't," she breathed.

Syris blinked, as if he struggled with the storm within him. His eyes snapped open wide and ablaze, seething with lust, with fear, with love.

And for the first time in all his existence, he did not turn away.

"You don't have to turn from this," Amara breathed. "You don't have to turn from me."

Syris finally looked her in the eyes, his golden eyes glinting in the moonlight. "I'm not running, Amara," he said, his voice husky. "I'm protecting you. Protecting myself."

"From what?" asked amara.

"From the sure hurt," he took a step back, breathing.

His loss had made him nervous, chilled and hollowed him out.

"Do you have any idea what it is to love something you never will? To catch something when you know it will always slip from your fingers?"

"Don't think of tomorrow. Don't think of what won't be. Just. be here. Now." said amara.

Syris snorted. "You make it sound so simple."

"Maybe it is," she told him.

"Maybe love isn't about sense, or reason, or prudence. Maybe it's purely a matter of feeling. And I feel you, Syris. I feel your pain, your phobias and your love." She said.

"Even if I do," he replied at last, "even if I let myself love you already, which I do, what then? What are we to do about it?" said syris.

"There is no definite future, Syris. But that never stopped me from having what my heart desires. " continued amara.

She touched him again, this time more forcefully, her hand tracing the fine feathers down the line of his jaw. "And my heart desires you."

Syris trembled beneath her fingers, between the love he had spurned all those centuries past and terror at what it would cost to take it.

"Amara..." he said.

She laughed, tears shining in her eyes. "Syris."

And in that instant, space did not exist between them.

Syris leaned into her touch, his determination shattering like fall leaves on the wind.

"I love you, Amara," he finally whispered, his voice shattered, fractured, but true. "But I am still afraid."

She leaned her forehead against him.

"Let me share your fear then. Let me carry it for you. Because love isn't living without fear, Syris. It's about loving each other in spite of the fear."

Syris breathed out, a burden lifted from his heart.

For the first time in his life, he permitted himself to believe.

Syris spread his wings slightly, coming closer to Amara.

"Then let us create our own tale," he said to her, his voice firm. "Even if the ending is uncertain."

Amara nodded, a lone tear running down her cheek—not of sadness, but of acceptance. They sat in friendly silence beneath the interminable extent, the stars above twinkle-blinky with promise of something yet unfulfilled.

Something neither of them had ever before dared to dream. And over this, the night breathed its blessing, conveying their silent vows upon the breezes up to the skies.

And eventually, it turned into a habit for Amara to offer Syris small mementos of affection—plump berries, flowers' fragrant petals, sweetness of nectar, or spring's wellspring water.

"Why are you making such an ado about this, Amara? It's not required. I am content with your affection," answered Syris in the afternoon, looking at her with wonder.

"Love does not grow out of need, Syris. It grows out of care," she answered softly with a smile.

That night, as part of their unofficial tradition, Amara sat under a tree and hummed quietly. Syris sat next to her—quiet, still. He didn't tweet, didn't talk—just remained close.

Amara felt him, she allowed the silence to build between them, warm and all-encompassing. She smiled to herself, knowing he was listening.

Syris observed her, understanding dawning—she knew him, even in silence. She left him alone, without expectation, without demand.

At that time, Syris gained something new from love. It wasn't merely spoken; it was felt. It was in the quiet, the waiting, the simple fact of being there.

For the first time, he didn't struggle against it. He no longer wanted to fly away.

Amara extended her hand cradling a handful of seeds. She didn't call out to him, didn't even look up—just waited.

Syris hesitated. His sharp eyes blazed with uncertainty. He had stolen from her hands before, but never so—so close, so exposed.

The movement was simple, but it felt like a bridge between them, one he had never been courageous enough to take.

His wings quivered, his heart pounded, but Amara did not stir, offering nothing but patience.

With a sigh, Syris stepped forward, his beak touching her palm as he took the initial seed. There was a moment suspended between them—one that was tenuous, but unbreakable.

Amara smiled faintly, and for the first time, Syris didn't recognize himself as a bird bound by fate. Unleashed, he felt.

"You never asked me to change, did you?" he breathed, his voice barely above the whisper of the wind.

Amara's head shook. "I just needed to tell you that you weren't alone."

The wind carried their unspoken promise—they together wherever. Stars started flickering above but Syris flew no place. He remained.

SEVEN

THE DILEMMA OF HEART

It was on one night as amara wandered across the serene country with Syris, his song of melodious sweetness filling the air.

He raved continuously about her—his love, his loyalty, his ever-abiding love. His words wrapped her in a comforting hold, but Amara was submerged in silence, lost in her own depths.

Noticing the shift, Syris turned toward her, sensing the unrest beneath her quiet demeanor.

"You're quiet," he remarked, his voice steady and calm.

Amara swallowed the lump in her throat and forced a small smile. "Just thinking."

Syris settled beside her, folding his great wings as his gaze lingered on the setting sun. "About what?"

She hesitated for a moment before she leaned in and whispered, "Ever wonder what it would be like... to be free?"

Syris leaned his head to one side. His golden eyes scanned hers.

"I am free, Amara."

Her breath suspended. "But if you were able to get out of this place—get out of me—would you?"

A soft laugh escaped him, as if the notion itself was absurd.

"Why would I? My home is here with you."

Her heart tightened. She thought, no, Syris. You have a place here where you ought to be. All his memories assaulted her brain, a reality she could not help but confront. But she could not disclose that to him.

She continued thinking about syris in her mind, how did I even imagine hurting you? How can I stand the thought of us apart? We are content in our own little universe, carefree. I have not even got the energy to mention it to you, Syris, for I know that you would never consent to departure and I am afraid, if I speak it out, that you won't get it.

You will be hurt or worse, turn against me.

The pressure of what wasn't being spoken weighed upon her chest, but all she could do was gaze at Syris, committing his face to memory, understanding that eventually, she'd be forced to make a decision—something that would alter the course of things.

She whispered to syris, "Syris, I never asked you for anything... but can I ask something now? Will you do me a favour?"

A low growl of laughter burst from him, his eyes warm as usual.

"You don't even need to ask. You just say it, and it's done."

Amara swallowed hard, hiding the tempest brewing inside of her. She would not let him see. Not yet. She laced an innocent note in her voice.

"It's no big thing. I just need you to trust me. Whatever comes."

Syris leaned toward her, taking note of her before he nodded.

"I do, already," he told her.

She flashed him a warm smile, and inside of herself, there seared the most painful throe of regret. If only he knew the privilege she was asking for, which he would never give her.

The wind sighed over the leaves as the sun dipped beneath the horizon, stretching long shadows over them. Amara turned away, catching the hem of her dress to steady herself. The time wasn't yet. But soon, it would be, and she would have to make a choice—for both of them.

Amara drew a deep breath, calming herself before continuing. "Syris, I must go away for a few days."

Syris immediately bristled, his eyes narrowing. "Leave? Where?"

She smiled, trying to sound casual, hoping he would not catch the trembling of her hands. "Just to see a distant relative. It won't be long."

Syris glared, his eyes fixed on her. "A relative? You've never said anything about them before."

Her heart racing, she would not give in. "I haven't seen them for years. It's something I have to do."

A flicker of doubt crossed his expression, but he nodded. "I don't want you to go alone."

She smiled, carefree on the outside but empty inside.

"You worry too much, Syris. I'll be fine."

His wings fluttered, his gold-coloured eyes still unsure.

"When will you be back?" he asked.

She paused before speaking, "Soon. Just give me a little time."

Syris let out a deep breath, not willing to but trusting.

"Alright... but promise me you'll be safe."

She nodded, producing another smile. "I promise."

But as she turned her back, her heart bled with the burden of truth. This wasn't a visit—it was a mission. A mission to reveal the truth behind Syris' curse... and how to release him from it.

Little did she know that the journey ahead would change everything.

EIGHT

PRICE OF FREEDOM AND PROMISE OF LOVE

Evening when Amara left, the sky wept as if mourning the weight of her unspoken truth. She wrapped her cloak tighter around her, her heart pounding in terror.

With each step away from Syris, it was betrayal to her soul, and yet she had known it was the only way for him.

She wandered through forests and waded across streams for days, traveling on the currents of ancient myths. She visited hidden temples in which the walls were covered in stories of trapped spirits on the plane of men.

She hunted wise men who replied in mystery and poets who wrote verse concerning lost souls suspended between realms.

Each answer led her to another, until she faced a shrine, far in the mountains, where time seems frozen.

An old lady with silver eyes sat next to a fire soldering, looking at Amara with a knowing gaze.

"You have come seeking a way to break his chains," the woman whispered before Amara could even get words out.

Amara swallowed. "Yes. Show me how to free him."

The woman stared at her for a minute before she shook her head. "To set free a soul that has grown used to its prison, you must make it believe there is no other choice but freedom."

Amara's brows were furrowed. "What are you saying?"

The woman sighed. "You must hurt him, child. Not his body, but his heart. You must make him believe you've betrayed him. Only through heartbreak will he sever the tie himself."

Amara's breath caught in her throat. "There must be another way.".

She smiled, though tragically. "Love is not always kind, my love. At times, it is an offering."

Amara's vision misted with tears, yet she nodded.

If this were the only solution to accomplish, she would walk through the pain. Even if Syris detested her for the rest of her life.

By the time she returned, the sun was setting, bathing the world in hues of gold and crimson.

Syris was waiting for her at the lake, his wings shimmering in the dying light. The moment he saw her, his face lit up with relief.

"You're back," he breathed, stepping closer. "I was starting to worry."

She forced a smile, but her hands trembled. "I brought something for you."

Walking in front of him, she displayed the silver feather she had laid at the centre of a magic rock circle.

She had been up all night preparing the spell, each rune drawn with trembling fingers, each spell of magic loaded with grief.

Syris tilted his head to one side. "What is this?"

"A gift," she breathed.

He stepped closer, his gold eyes glinting with trust as he extended his hand for the feather. As soon as his fingers touched, the circle flared to life. A burst of golden light erupted at his feet, holding him fast.

His wings flapped wildly in terror. "Amara?"

She folded her fists, her heart pounding. "This is the truth, Syris. You were never supposed to remain here."

His face fixed, his tone icy with incredulity. "You're lying."

"I'm not." She regulated her voice calm, though her heart was bleeding with pain. "You're a trapped spirit, Syris. And I'm the one who's held you captive here."

His wings quivered, his eyes broad with outrage. "You did this to me?"

The magic enveloped him, holding him in place, his body shaking under the pressure. Pain flashed across his face.

"Amara, stop!" His voice was now desperate. "Please! Don't do this to me!"

She turned away, not wanting to see what was in his eyes.

"Goodbye, Syris." she murmured.

With a final chant, the spell cut the final connection. A scream was ripped from Syris' body as the golden light engulfed him, his body breaking down into energy.

And then, he disappeared.

Amara sank down onto the earth, sobbing. He was free. And why should she think she'd lost something fundamental?

The wind changed, bringing with it a blast of warmth. And then, out of vanishing mist, formation. A man, in white robes that rippled like water, his golden eyes filled with some unreadable something.

Her breath held. "Syris?"

He looked at her, his own face blank. "You lied to me."

She swallowed, her whisper almost inaudible. "I had to."

He lay still for a moment that seemed like an eternity. And then he reached out and touched her, his fingers outlining the shape of her cheek with tortured tenderness.

"You gave me my freedom... at the price of your own heart." asked syris.

Her tears spilled over, but she gazed at him. "I would do it again."

He still wore a hurt smile on his lips. "I thought you betrayed me. I thought you would hurt me." He breathed deeply, shaking his head from side to side.

"But you loved me more than anyone." he confessed.

She jutted out her lip, not wanting to ask the question that was driving her heart crazy. "So this means. I'll never be able to see you any longer?"

His smile relaxed. "You will see me constantly."

Her eyebrow furrowed. "What are you telling me?"

Syris stepped back, his body shuddering like the dying sunbeams. "Where you need me, there I will be. Perhaps as a bird, perhaps as some human. But I will find you."

Her heart twisted. "Syris..."she said.

His golden eyes burned with vow. "Because love such as this does not die."

And he was gone on the wind, leaving nothing behind but a moonlight-glancing silver feather.

Amara clutched it to her heart and wept. She did not know when or how, but she did know—he would come back.

For love never quite lets go.

NINE
ETERNAL WHISPERS

The rain scent filled the air, gentle patter of rain on the windowsill as Amara sat in solitude in her small house.

Her fingers tracing the edges of a yellowed canvas, colours faded but emotions still present. It was a work that she had used to create—a painting of golden wings spread in the protection of a twilight sky, a part of her soul trapped forever.

Tears streamed down her face as all the memories flooded back into her mind. The manner in which Syris had looked at her, the warmth that had radiated from his very presence, the unsaid words still lingering between them.

She had released him, but the emptiness in her heart never dissipated.

As if answering to keep up with her sorrow, the soft chirping trembled the quiet.

Amara waved her hand over her eyes and looked toward the open window.

Perched comfortably there, lying elegantly on the wood sill, was a gold-plumed bird the size of her hand.

Her gasp.

That melody. She had heard that melody.

"Is it, you?" she breathed, not standing, not thinking.

The bird cocked his head, golden eyes filled with warmth and a smile she knew all too well. And then, for her alone, started to shine, his form fluid, expanding into something more.

In the space of another heartbeat, Syris stood in front of her, as ever she'd known him—eyes burning golden full of something boundless and unshattered.

"Did you really think I would leave you?" he breathed.

She burst out in tears hugging him firmly, encasing him in a grip of arms. He stood before her, warm and heavy and real—just as he always was.

"I missed you," she murmured on his chest.

He smoothed a hand through her hair, the strands soft and silky. "I never went anywhere, Amara."

She eased back away from him by an inch, her face uplifted to his, and voice tremulous.

"But you were free. Why did you come back?"

He grinned, a characteristic glint in his eye. "Because freedom isn't departure—it's choosing where home is. And I am home with you."

Amara's heart was afire with feeling, but before she could respond, soft gold began to radiate from him, golden and warm.

Syris cupped her hands in the bowl of his, cradling something into the bowl of her hand. She gazed down and discovered a slender pendant, shining like the sun rising at dawn.

" This is me," he breathed.

"My essence, my heart. I did it freely, Amara. Not a prisoner of destiny in spirit, but a guardian, at your side, always." he said.

Teardrops sparkled on the edges of her eyes as she fastened the pendant to the centre of her chest.

"You mean."

He nodded.

"When you require me, I shall be there. A wind to stir in the breeze, the warmth of an arm against flesh, a voice which will not leave.".

About The Author

Shivangi Goswami is a passionate storyteller who weaves fantasy and romance into unforgettable tales of love, destiny, and magic. With a deep love for mythology and mystical worlds, she brings to life characters who defy fate and embrace the extraordinary.

When she's not writing, she enjoys exploring folklore, dreaming up new adventures, and connecting with readers who share her love for enchanting stories. Bound by Feathers, Freed by Love is her debut novel, marking the beginning of many more magical journeys to come.

Connect with Shivangi:
Email :- shivangigoswami311@gmail.com
Instagram :- @talesbyshivangi